The Crown

Praise for Storyshares

"One of the brightest innovators and game-changers in the education industry."
– Forbes

"Your success in applying research-validated practices to promote literacy serves as a valuable model for other organizations seeking to create evidence-based literacy programs."
- Library of Congress

"We need powerful social and educational innovation, and Storyshares is breaking new ground. The organization addresses critical problems facing our students and teachers. I am excited about the strategies it brings to the collective work of making sure every student has an equal chance in life."
– Teach For America

"It's the perfect idea. There's really nothing like this. I mean, wow, this will be a wonderful experience for young people."
- Andrea Davis Pinkney, Executive Director, Scholastic

"Reading for meaning opens opportunities for a lifetime of learning. Providing emerging readers with engaging texts that are designed to offer both challenges and support for each individual will improve their lives for years to come. Storyshares is a wonderful start."
- David Rose, Co-founder of CAST & UDL

The Crown

Sydney Osterday

A Storyshares book

Published by Story Share, Inc.

Storyshares

Story Share, Inc.

24 N. Bryn Mawr Avenue #340

Bryn Mawr, PA 19010-3304

www.storyshares.org

Inspiring reading with a new kind of book.

Interest Level: Late Elementary

Grade Level Equivalent: 0.8

9781642613254

Book design by Storyshares

Storyshares Presents

Chapter One

The Essay

IT WAS MONDAY. THE day my class would learn the topic of the essay.

Would I fail or succeed? I wondered.

"Okay, class," Mrs. Thomas said. "You are going to write an essay."

Tony raised his hand. It was too early to ask a question.

"Yes, Tony?" Mrs. Thomas asked.

"What's the essay supposed to be about?" he asked.

She smiled at him. She knew what everyone was waiting for, but she held out. She wanted us to wait, to learn patience.

"The essay topic," she said, "is to write about who you are and who you want to be."

I smiled. I knew I could write an essay that would impress Mrs. Thomas.

I pulled out a piece of paper and a pen. I was about to start writing, but then I stopped.

Who was I, really? I thought. *Was I the smart person? Was I the shy person? Was I the funny person?*

I thought long and hard about the essay.

I didn't *know* who I was.

After class, I went up to Mrs. Thomas's desk to ask her about the essay.

"Mrs. Thomas, I'm not sure what to write," I said.

She looked up at me and smiled.

"Well, think about it for the next few days," she said. "If you still can't write, then I can give you something else to write about."

"Okay, thank you," I said.

I would not give up. I was going to write the essay about who I was, even if it took all night. I had the writing skills. I just needed to find out what I wanted to say.

I walked to the door.

"Bye, Mrs. Thomas," I called back to her.

"Goodbye, Bailey. Have a nice day," she said.

I left the classroom and walked home without saying a word. I was thinking about the essay. I would not be able to think about anything else until it was done.

Chapter Two

Who Am I?

I STOPPED AT MY house and told my parents I was going for a walk. Then I put on my tennis shoes and headed out. I was going to the woods to think about the essay. The sounds of nature would calm me and help me to think.

The woods were close to my house. I walked down the street, turned left, then turned left again. There was a small trail that started at the sidewalk. It went on for miles through the woods.

I passed the old sign with the words 'Fang Trail" on it.

My trip to find out who I am was just beginning.

I would write the essay. I would not let myself down. I *could not* let Mrs. Thomas down.

I walked the trail into the forest. I only brought a pen. I could write notes on my hand when I thought of ideas.

The forest was dark. The trees blocked out most of the sunlight. I did not mind. As long as I could see the trail, I was fine.

"Hello!" I yelled into the forest.

Birds in the trees woke from their sleep. They chirped and flew into the air. I loved their chirps.

The birds' calls woke other animals. Soon, all the animals were calling out. The forest wasn't quiet anymore. It was full of sound.

I ran down the trail. I ran so fast that not even a horse could have caught me. I ran and ran. I ran until my lungs hurt. Then I fell onto the grass next to the trail.

I rolled onto my back and stared up at the sky.

Who am I? I thought.

I still could not answer the question.

"Who are *you?*" I asked the forest.

I knew the forest would not answer me. But I knew who the forest was, anyway. It was animals, plants, and dirt. It was chirps and grass and trees. It was life.

I knew who the forest was, but I did not know who *I* was.

"Who am I?" I asked the forest again.

The forest would not tell me. I listened to the sounds of the animals, but they did not tell me either.

I stood up. I wiped the grass off my clothes. No one would tell me who I was, so I had to find out for myself.

I started walking down the trail again. The forest got darker and darker as I went. I stopped. There was a tunnel made out of leaves and branches.

I ran from the trail and down the tunnel. It seemed to go on forever. I ran even faster when I saw a light at the end of it.

I had to crawl through the small opening. The light was so bright. I could not see where I was going.

I kept crawling until I was out of the tunnel. Then I stood up. I blinked until I could see again.

I gasped.

I had crawled to the most beautiful place I had ever seen.

I was standing in a grassy spot in the middle of the forest. The trees around me were huge. They looked more than a hundred feet tall.

Butterflies in every color flew through the air. They were blue, purple, yellow, and even green.

Small red and yellow birds sat on every tree branch. They sang cheerful songs.

Rabbits hopped through the grass. Squirrels jumped from branch to branch. Moles popped out of their holes. There was even a deer, hiding in the trees.

I had never seen this part of the forest before. It was so beautiful. I smiled with joy.

I stopped looking around at the trees when a sound came from the forest. The trees in front of me shook. The ground under me shook. I was afraid of what would come out of the forest.

Suddenly, the biggest group of rabbits I had ever seen came running from the trees. They weren't moving on four legs, but on two. And they were bigger than rabbits should be. They were almost as tall as me!

The ground shook harder. I fell down. The large rabbits were coming right at me. I did the only thing I could do.

"Help!" I screamed.

I sat on the ground and hid my face. I waited for the rabbits to run right over me, but they did not. All I could feel was air going by me.

I looked up. The rabbits were running around me. They looked like small, furry humans up close.

I sat still until the rabbits had all run past me. Then one rabbit came walking out of the forest, last. The group had left him. He was having a hard time breathing. He bent over and grabbed his knees. "Hello?" I said.

Chapter Three
Ralph

THE RABBIT LOOKED UP.

I laughed. It wasn't a rabbit at all. It was a man in a bunny outfit.

He walked up to me.

"Hi," he said.

"Why are you wearing that silly outfit?" I asked.

He looked down at his costume and frowned.

"Silly? My outfit is not silly!" he said angrily.

He was a foot taller than me and looked about seventeen years old.

I stood up. I crossed my arms over my chest.

"Fine," I said. "Then why are you wearing that outfit that *definitely* does not look silly on a grown boy."

He frowned again, but he didn't get mad.

"Well, if you must know, I'm not really a Wabooz Rabbit," he said.

"I'm a human hiding from—"

"A Wabooz Rabbit?" I interrupted. "There is no such thing."

"Of course there is! What did you think those animals were? Normal rabbits?" he asked.

"What else would they be, other than rabbits?" I asked. I was getting angry now.

He laughed. "You really aren't very smart," he said.

He was not being very nice.

"And who were you hiding from?" I asked.

"Who was I hiding from?" he repeated with a smile.

He broke out laughing. He rolled onto the grass and kicked his legs.

I just stood there while he laughed and laughed. I was angry that he laughed at me.

I turned to go back through the tunnel, but it was gone! I looked around, but there were only trees. I turned around to look for the tunnel again. I saw nothing.

I was lost!

Soon, I gave up looking for the way I came here. It was no use. The tunnel was gone.

I started walking. I would probably never find my way back to the trail, but I could try.

"Hey! Wait! Where are you going?" the bunny asked.

I turned back. He ran up in front of me. I was happy that he had stopped laughing.

"I'm going home," I said.

"Wait, what animal are you?" he asked.

"I'm a girl," I said.

"A girl! I thought I would never see another girl! Tell me, how did you get here?" he asked. "We can go back the way you came and get home! I have been stuck here for a very long time."

"I came here through a tunnel and now it is gone! There's no way back!" I yelled at him.

He frowned. He sat down on the ground, looking upset.

"I am never going to get home," he said.

"Do not be sad," I told him. "We will find a way to get you home." I patted his back.

He looked up at me and smiled. He hopped to his feet.

"You are right. Let's get going!" he said.

He was a very moody rabbit.

"Where?" I asked.

"To the place where everyone goes when they need to find something!" he said.

Chapter Four

The Lost Library

"AND WHERE IS THAT?" I asked.

"The Lost Library," he said.

He motioned for me to follow him.

I walked behind him through the forest.

"Well, if it is lost, how are we going to find it?" I asked.

"We cannot," he said.

"What?" I asked.

How were we going to find a library that was lost and could not be found? I wondered.

He looked back at me and smiled.

"The Lost Library finds *you*," he said. "We just have to keep going until it does."

I stopped walking.

He turned around. He frowned at me.

"You mean you don't know where we're going?" I yelled at him.

"That's not what I said," he said.

If he could not find The Lost Library, then how would he know where to go? Nothing made sense.

"I have this," he said.

He pulled out a necklace from under his outfit. It was a locket.

When he opened it, there was a compass inside.

"This compass tells me where to go to find The Lost Library," he said. "The problem is that the library is always moving. But if we hurry, we can catch up with it."

"What do you mean, it's always moving?" I asked.

"You will see," he said.

He turned and started walking again.

I walked behind him. I did not know if we would *ever* find The Lost Library.

We walked for hours. I was starting to get hungry.

"Can we take a break?" I asked.

"No, we cannot stop now. We are almost there," he said.

"How do you know that we are almost there?" I asked.

"I can feel it," he said.

All I could feel was my stomach growling.

"I didn't get your name," he said.

"It's Bailey," I said.

"Bailey. Hmm," he said.

"What? Is there something wrong with my name?" I asked.

"Nope, it just makes me think of someone," he said. "Oh, and my name is Ralph."

"Well, Ralph—" I started to say.

I was cut off by a loud sound in the forest.

Ralph stopped. I bumped into his back.

"What's going on?" I asked.

"We are here," he said. He leaned back to me and added, "You should be careful. The bookkeeper is a vampire."

"A vampire!" I gasped.

I grabbed my neck. No one was going to suck my blood.

"No, silly," Ralph said. "He only eats hearts."

I gulped. That was worse.

Ralph grabbed my arm and pulled me along with him. We ran toward the loud sound.

It was a huge bug, as big as a house. It crashed through the trees as it walked. Its skin was a shiny black.

I was scared to go near it.

I tried to pull my arm away from Ralph, but I could not. He was too strong.

Ralph ran up to the large bug and hit its side.

"Open up, Charlie!" he yelled.

The bug's mouth opened and its tongue rolled out. Its spit made the ground wet.

I frowned. I felt grossed out.

Ralph stepped onto its tongue and held his hand out to me.

I shook my head. I was not going to be eaten by a bug.

"Come on... Please?" he said.

I paused, then finally gave in. I needed to get home, even if that meant getting eaten by a huge bug. I stepped onto the tongue.

We walked up the tongue and into the bug's insides. We moved into the darkness.

Ralph pulled me along with him. When he yelled and fell down, I did too. We went sliding down a long tube. It must have been the bug's throat. We shot out of the end and hit the soft ground below.

I stood up from the floor and wiped the dirt from my shirt. Ralph was already walking deeper into the bug's insides.

We were now in a dark room lit by lamps. There were rows and rows of bookshelves. It would have taken me at least twenty years to read all the books in that room.

I ran over to where Ralph had gone.

A tall man stood in front of him. The man had dark hair and black eyes. He smiled at me and two white fangs showed.

I gulped. This must be the vampire.

"Hello," the vampire said. "What can I help you with?"

"We need to get home," Ralph said.

"Home?" the vampire asked.

"Back to the human world," I said.

"Oh, I see. I know what you need," the vampire said.We followed behind the vampire until he stopped. He grabbed a large book and pulled it down from the shelf.

"Here you go," the vampire said.

He gave the book to Ralph.

I looked at it. It was old and dusty. I started to ask how the book would help us, but I was cut off.

A slimy rope grabbed onto my waist. It also grabbed Ralph.

"Bye-bye for now," the vampire said.

I screamed as Ralph and I were flung backwards. We went flying up the bug's throat and fell down its tongue. We landed in the grass.

Before I could get to my feet, the bug closed its mouth and took off. It walked into the forest and out of sight.

I stood up. Ralph hopped to his feet and grabbed the large book from the ground. Then he turned and started walking.

"Come on," he said.

"Wait! I need to rest," I said.

He looked back at me. "I know," he said. "We will go to Blue Belly Pond and rest."

I was so tired. My legs hurt from walking. Still, I walked along behind Ralph until we came to a clear, blue pond deep in the woods.

Chapter Five

Blue Belly Pond and The Book of Evils

THE POND WAS SO clear and so blue that it did not really look like a pond.

I ran to the water to get a drink. Before I could get there, something knocked me back. I fell onto my back in the grass.

Ralph ran over and helped me up.

"Are you crazy?" he asked. "People are not supposed to drink from Blue Belly Pond!"

"How was I supposed to know that?" I asked.

A head popped out of the water and said, "Read the sign."

I gasped.

It could not be real, I thought.

But it was. A mermaid. She lay across the rocks in the middle of the pond. Her tail splashed in the clear, blue water.

Another mermaid came up and sat next to her. One had dark hair and the other had gold hair. Their tails were covered in shiny blues and greens. They were very pretty.

"Mermaids!" I gasped. I still could not believe it.

"Do not let them fool you," Ralph said. "They are not all that great."

"Oh, Ralph," the mermaid with the golden hair said. "You cannot still be mad about the other day."

Both of the mermaids giggled. They flipped their hair and smiled sweetly.

"What happened the other day?" I asked.

"Nothing," Ralph said with a frown.

"We just played a trick on him," the mermaid with golden hair said.

"Oh, yes, just a silly trick," the mermaid with dark hair said.

They both giggled again.

I did not know what was so funny.

"Okay," I said, ignoring them. "Ralph, let's look at the book."

"Oh, yeah," he said.

We sat down on a log near the pond and looked at the front cover. The title was *The Book of Evils.*

"Evils as in what?" I asked.

"As in bad things that you should be scared of," Ralph said.

"Great," I said.

I grabbed the edge of the cover and started to open the book.

"Wait," Ralph said.

"What?" I asked.

"I think Ron marked the page for us," he said.

"The vampire guy?" I asked.

"Yes, the vampire guy," he answered.

Ralph opened to the page with the bookmark in it. It was filled with a picture of a scary woman.

Her eyes were dark green. She had dirty hair. Her clothes were made of leaves and branches. The caption above the picture read

"Alroon, The Evil Wood Fairy."

"What's an evil wood fairy? And what does it have to do with getting home?" I asked.

"It is very smart," Ralph said. "It lives in the woods and plays tricks on anyone who goes near it."

"Okay, but how can this evil wood fairy help us get home?" I asked.

I waited for Ralph to read through the writing under the picture.

One part was written in a weird language that I did not understand.

"It says here," he said, pointing at the weird text, "that we need to take the fairy's crown."

"What? Why?" I asked.

"The fairy's crown can take you anywhere you want to go. It is a key that unlocks worlds," he said.

"Okay, so how do we take it?" I asked.

"Oh, Ralph, do you need help getting rid of a silly old fairy?" the golden haired mermaid called to us.

She was on the edge of the pond now.

"No, I am not in the mood for your tricks," he said. "Now be nice and go get us some food and water."

The mermaid sighed. "If I must," she said.

She went under the water. The other mermaid was still lying on the rocks, but she jumped off and followed.

"Look here," Ralph said.

He pointed to the page. It said we needed "Giant tears and Red Weeds."

"Giant tears? How are we supposed to get that? And what are Red Weeds?" I asked.

"I know where the Giants live, but I do not know what Red Weeds are. I will ask the mermaids," Ralph said.

Just then, the golden-haired mermaid popped up. She had a flat rock with four shells on it. Two shells had white meat and the other two had a sip of water.

I was so thirsty that I did not think a sip of water would be enough.

"Thanks," Ralph said.

He grabbed the rock from the mermaid. Then he walked back to the log and sat down next to me.

He picked up the shell and drank the water. Then he ate the small chunk of white meat.

I did the same. I was shocked to find that the water and meat filled me up. I was no longer hungry or thirsty.

Ralph looked tired. His eyes closed and he fell to the ground.

Then I started to feel tired. My eyes drooped closed. I fell beside him and went to sleep.

Chapter Six

The Mermaid's Trick and The Red Weeds

"BAILEY, WAKE UP," A voice said.

I sighed and opened my eyes.

I was on the ground where I'd fallen asleep. Ralph helped me to my feet. I still felt tired.

"What happened?" I asked.

"The mermaids played a trick on us. They put something in our food," he said angrily.

Just then, a mermaid head popped out of the water.

"Good morning, sleepyheads," the golden-haired mermaid said.

Ralph's face turned red. He opened his mouth to yell.

"You—" he started to call, but the mermaid cut him off.

"I know, Ralph. I am sorry for playing a trick on you again. It is just fun to see you angry. I will make it up to you," she said.

"How?" Ralph asked.

"I happen to have some Red Weeds," she said.

Her hand lifted out of the water. She was holding a small, red plant.

Ralph looked less angry.

"All right, I cannot be mad at you now," he said.

The mermaid giggled. She dropped the Red Weeds at the edge of the pond and went under the water.

Ralph walked over and grabbed the Red Weeds. He put them in the front pocket of his outfit.

"Come on," he said. "We are done here."

I walked along behind Ralph.

"Where are we going?" I asked.

"To the Giant's home," he said.

I gulped. The bug was scary, but a Giant would be even scarier.

"When do Giants cry?" I asked.

"Never," he said.

"Then how are we supposed to make them cry?" I asked.

"I don't know," Ralph said. "Why do you think I have all the answers?"

"You have known every answer so far," I said.

"Well, there's a first time for everything," he said.

"What's wrong? Are you mad at me?" I asked.

"No. Just don't talk until we get there," he said.

"Okay," I said.

I hoped I had not made him angry. It was so nice of him to help me get home.

The part of the forest we were walking in was dark. I was scared, but I was not supposed to talk. I could not tell Ralph I was afraid.

We walked for an hour before we got to a dark, brick path. We went on the path for a long time. I was starting to get hungry again when we finally reached a bridge.

Ralph turned to me and said, "I am sorry for being rude. The mermaids just put me in a bad mood."

"That's okay," I said.

"The Giants live under the bridge," he said.

"Got a plan?" I asked.

"Nope," he said.

Before I could ask him anything else, Ralph walked up to the bridge.

A huge man came up onto it. He stood in the center. He looked almost twenty feet tall. He had a big nose and black eyes.

Chapter Seven
The Giants and Their Tears

THE GROUND SHOOK AND two more Giants came up onto the bridge. They were smelly and scary.

"Who dares cross our bridge?" the biggest one asked.

"We do not want to cross your bridge," Ralph said.

"Then what do you want?" the biggest Giant asked.

"We want to talk," Ralph said. "About the dark times."

"Why do you want to know about the dark times?" the Giant yelled.

His voice made a strong wind. I could barely stay standing.

Ralph's plan was not working. He was making the Giants angry, not sad.

"I want to know about how you lost Green Bridge to a group of kids," Ralph said.

This made all the Giants angrier. They stomped their feet. The ground shook. Ralph and I fell onto the ground.

The biggest Giant grabbed Ralph and picked him up.

"You should know not to make Giants angry!" the Giant yelled.

He lifted Ralph higher into the air.

"Stop!" I screamed.

The Giant froze.

I got to my feet and walked up to the bridge.

"Put him down!" I yelled.

The Giant laughed. "Why?" he asked.

"You know what?" I said. "Do what you want."

I was upset and angry. Ralph's plan had made a mess. A mess that I did not know how to fix.

"I just went to the woods to find out who I am. Now I am in this crazy world and I cannot get home. I am lost and scared. And you are trying to hurt my only friend," I said. "I just want to go home and see my mom and dad."

Tears ran down my cheeks.

The Giant set Ralph down next to me.

"I don't know why you have to be so mean. We did not want to hurt you," I said.

The biggest Giant bent down in front of me.

"Don't cry," he said. "I am sorry for making you upset."

I could not stop crying. I did not know if I would ever get home.

The Giant's eyes also filled with tears. Soon, all the Giants were crying with me.

"We are sorry!" they sobbed.

Ralph grabbed a jar out of his outfit pocket. He ran up under the Giants and got a tear in the jar just before it hit the ground.

I hugged the Giant around its neck. They were being nice now, but they still smelled bad.

I dried my eyes. So did the Giants.

"We are sorry," the biggest Giant said again.

"It's okay," I told him.

The Giant reached into his pocket. He gave me a large chunk of bread.

"Here you go," he said.

Then the biggest Giant picked us up and set us on the other side of the bridge.

"Thank you!" I called to them all.

They waved goodbye as we walked off into the forest.

"Well played," Ralph said.

"I wasn't playing," I said.

"Anyway, well done," he said.

We ate the large chunk of bread. Then we fell asleep on a pile of leaves in the shade.

Chapter Eight
The Lizard Queen

I WOKE UP AND looked around. Ralph was gone. I began to worry.

What if he wanted the crown for himself? I thought. *What if he'd been taken?*

I stood up and looked around for him.

There was something pink on the ground. I walked over to it.

Ralph's bunny hood. It was ripped and dirty. Something must have grabbed him when we were sleeping.

I reached for the hood and went to look for Ralph. I did not know if I was going the right way. I only knew that I had to find him.

I walked for twenty minutes. I was worried. I still hadn't seen him.

I kept going until I heard voices up ahead. Then I bent down and ran to a bush. I hid there and looked at the people standing in the small clearing ahead.

Ralph was there! His hands were tied behind his back. He was on the ground, facing a tall, pretty woman.

Her scaly skin changed colors as she moved. She was just like a lizard. She had light blue eyes.

She held a large wooden stick that sparkled in the light.

"Ralph," she said. "You have hidden from me for long enough. You broke my heart. You hurt me, so you must pay."

She closed her eyes. The wooden stick began to glow. When she opened her eyes again, they were red. She pointed the stick at Ralph.

This could not be good.

I ran out into the clearing.

"Stop!" I screamed.

The woman's eyes went back to blue. She set the wooden stick down.

"Who are you?" she asked. "And why do you care about this terrible man?"

I opened my mouth to say something, but she cut me off.

"Is this your new love? Have you moved on already?" she screamed at Ralph.

I wanted to tell her that Ralph and I were friends, but I had a feeling she wouldn't care.

Her eyes turned red and her wooden stick began to glow once more. She pointed it at me.

Just then, Ralph broke out of the rope tied around his hands. He jumped up and grabbed the wooden stick from the woman. He pointed it at her.

A red light shot from the end. The woman blew up in a cloud of ash.

I screamed.

"Ralph!" I yelled. "What did you do?"

He dropped the stick and looked at me. He had a black eye and a cut on his chin.

"I... I..." he said.

I ran to Ralph and grabbed him in a hug.

I knew the woman was evil. I knew she was going to hurt him. I was so happy that he was alive. I didn't care about anything else.

We pulled out of the hug and stepped back from each other.

"We need to hurry and get you home," he said.

"What about you?" I asked.

"I have to do some stuff before I leave," he said. "I came here with my sister, many years ago. I need to find her before I go home."

"I can help you find your sister. Then we can all go home together," I said.

"No," he said. "It is best to go home when you can. The longer you are here, the harder it is to leave."

At last, I gave in.

"Okay," I said. "I'll go."

Chapter Nine
The Evil Wood Fairy, Alroon

"Do you need to rest?" I asked Ralph.

"No, I am okay," he said.

I was worried about Ralph, but he wanted to get to the crown. I was not going to fight him.

"Where to?" I asked.

"The woods next to Gray Creek. She should be there," he said.

"Okay," I said.

"I put the Red Weeds and Giant tears in a jar," he said. "Just put some of it on the fairy. That should put her to sleep, so we can take her crown."

He gave me the jar with the red tears.

"Do you think this will work?" I asked.

"If it doesn't work, then we might not get away from her," he said.

I gulped. Putting some of the red tears on the fairy was going to be hard. The fairy would probably do anything to keep her crown. If the crown could take me home, then it must be powerful. The fairy would not want to lose it.

We walked for a few more hours before coming to Gray Creek.

"Now what?" I asked.

"We wait," Ralph said.

He sat down next to the creek. I sat next to him.

He opened his mouth and began to sing.

"What are you doing?" I asked.

"Fairies hate singing more than anything else. I am going to bring her to us," he said.

He broke out in song:

"Oh, good fortune,
Take me home,
Take me to the home I love,
Bring me happiness,
Bring me joy,
Keep me under your wing,
Oh, good fortune,
Come to me..."
Ralph only stopped singing when there was a sound above us.
We both looked up and there she was.

Her flower crown sparkled in the sunlight. She looked down at us with dark green eyes. Her dark hair hung around her. She swung on a tree branch and dropped to the ground next to us.

"Why, hello there, little ones. Come to steal my crown?" she asked, laughing.

I did not know what to say. How did she know we wanted her crown?

I looked over at Ralph. He was calm. I didn't know how he wasn't scared.

She looked deep into my eyes. I started to feel dizzy. Her laughter was all around me. I fell to the ground. I let go of the jar with the red tears.

I did not know if Ralph was all right. I could not see him. All I could see was Alroon's face. It spun around me, faster and faster.

I was so scared. I didn't use the red tears.

The plan didn't work.

Chapter Ten

Going Home

BLACKNESS WAS ALL AROUND me. I thought I fell asleep, but I wasn't sure.

I opened my eyes.

I was in my room. Both of my parents were next to my bed.

"Oh, Bailey. I'm so happy you are all right," my mom said.

"What happened?" I asked.

"We found you sleeping in the woods," my dad said. "With that crown on your head."

He pointed at Alroon's crown. It was real, and sitting next to my bed.

"Ralph!" I gasped.

"Who's Ralph?" my mom asked.

"Uh... No one," I said. "Wait, what day is it?"

"It's Monday. Monday morning," my mom said.

"Monday!" I gasped. "I need to go to school!"

"Just stay home and rest. You can go to school tomorrow," my dad said.

"No, I need to go today," I said.

"Well, all right," my mom said. "Get dressed and I will meet you in the car."

I got ready as fast as I could and went to the car. I was happy my mom was driving me, but I was upset that I didn't get to write my essay.

I asked my mom to hurry.

We made it to school just in time for classes to start. My face turned bright red when everyone but me turned in their essays.

After class, I went up to Mrs. Thomas's desk. I told her I needed something else to write about. I had the rest of my life to find out who I was. I didn't need to know right now.

Instead, I got to write an essay about a dream. I wrote about my time with Ralph in the place in the woods.

Mrs. Thomas loved it. She said I made the place seem real.

Chapter Eleven
Old Friends

I WAS WALKING HOME from school that Friday when I heard someone calling my name.

I turned around to see Ralph! He was standing next to... Alroon?

I ran up to him.

"What—" I started to ask.

"Let me explain," he said. "I realized that the fairy was my sister. After you dropped the jar, I grabbed it. I put the red tears on her and she turned back to her old self. Then I put the crown on you and it took you home."

"So, how did you get home?" I asked.

"Now, that's another story," he said. He laughed.

"Well, I don't care how you got here," I said. "I am just happy that you are here."

He turned to his sister. "This is Ally," he said.

I shook her hand. She smiled at me.

"Nice to meet you," I said.

"Nice to meet you, too," she said.

"I'm going to wait in the car," Ally said to Ralph.

"Okay," he said.

I waved goodbye to her.

"Where are you staying?" I asked.

"At our parents' house, a few miles away from here," he said. "I can visit anytime, if you would like that?"

"Of course I would like that!" I said.

"Great! Here is my number," he said.

He handed me a slip of paper.

"Thanks," I said. I smiled.

"I have to go, but call me anytime. Tonight, even," he said.

"Okay, I will," I promised.

Before walking away, he grabbed me in a tight hug. He kissed me on my cheek and then let go of me.

I watched him walk back to his car with a smile on my face.

All I could think about was how he looked better without the bunny outfit.

About the Author

Sydney Osterday is a contributing author to the Storyshares library.

About the Publisher

Story Shares is a nonprofit focused on supporting the millions of teens and adults who struggle with reading by creating a new shelf in the library specifically for them. The ever-growing collection features content that is compelling and culturally relevant for teens and adults, yet still readable at a range of lower reading levels.

Story Shares generates content by engaging deeply with writers, bringing together a community to create this new kind of book. With more intriguing and approachable stories to choose from, the teens and adults who have fallen behind are improving their skills and beginning to discover the joy of reading. For more information, visit storyshares.org.

Easy to Read. Hard to Put Down.

Notes

www.ingramcontent.com/pod-product-compliance
Lightning Source LLC
Chambersburg PA
CBHW071229170626
46809CB00005BA/1991